# BLACK SMOKE AND BLIND MEN

BY DAN PINGER

ISBN: 978-0-9980991-3-2
First Edition

# ACKNOWLEDGMENTS

My dear young granddaughters, Eve and Ama Keller, are the inspiration for this book. At the time of publishing just one and two years old, they are the future of this fragile planet and will face the realities of the environmental damage earlier generations have inflicted. My deepest gratitude also goes to their grandmother, Debra Pinger, my friend, Bob Kraft, and my daughter, Ellen DePodesta, all of whom provided vital editing support for this book, along with excellent counsel. Further, Ellen, my partner in this project, was also responsible for the books publishing mechanics as well as the creative treatment of its covers.

My love also goes to my other children, Judy Pinger, Dan Pinger Jr., Karen Winkler, Alex Keller, and Cora Keller; to Will Colwell; and to my grown grandchildren Annika and Ryan Winkler.

I am continually grateful for the wise advice and vision provided to me by my dear friend and acclaimed author Ann Hagedorn, and for the daily care bestowed on me and my nine horses atop Ripley Ridge by Dan Hanshaw and Linda South.

# TABLE OF CONTENTS

# CHAPTER 1

## 26 YEARS AFTER OUR WORLD CAME TO A FIERY END

I stood, flabbergasted.

A stranger, who introduced himself as Captain Cos, just dropped by cable into my canyon, a place of hot, thin, dry, burned air. He was wearing an astronaut's suit of silvery blue, spoke in perfect English, and said he is from the planet Aura.

He and his team of scientists had come to Earth nine months ago searching for any form of life while testing air qualities and temperatures. They had cruised multi-thousands of miles of sandy and pebbled desert. Just before their scheduled departure, they discovered my harsh, deep gorge of dirty red, grey, and black jagged rocks.

Captain Cos's eyes were steady; his smile bright, skin ivory, physically fit, tall and slender.

"My God, man, how have you survived?" He seemed as shocked to see me as I was to see him.

I pointed to my tiny bubbling spring and the berries surrounding it, my now tattered encyclopedia, my dictionary, and my semblance of a backpack.

"You must be the only person left on Earth," he exclaimed. We sat on large rocks and talked.

"All I know is I was alone one day on my farmhouse porch outside the village of Ripley, Ohio. I was ten years old and at the beginning of shaping my thoughts. I had just returned from school with that backpack tightly strapped to my shoulders. Suddenly, it became unbearably hot. I never had known such heat. It was sweltry, followed by horrendous winds that were flaring and blazing. In a flash, there was fire everywhere. Our house, barns and animals were swept up and twisted in the air. Everything that stayed on the ground became ash. I was sucked into a tornado cylinder that spun around and around and was finally dropped into this canyon."

"Were you hurt?"

"I knew immediately my left arm and fingers were broken," I told him. "I hurt all over. I had knots on my head. I stayed still, eventually scooting over so that my right hand could reach for berries and to cup water. Otherwise, I do not know how I would have survived."

"It has been a constant fight with boredom. In my backpack, I still had an encyclopedia, an English dictionary and a note from my mom saying, 'Be home by six'. I must have reread that note thousands of times. I felt her love from wherever she is now.

"I've lost all sense of time," I said. "You say it has been 26 years? Where were you then?"

He said, "I was in my mother's womb. But I certainly know a lot about the apocalypse – that's what we call it. Every day of my life I have heard something about it.

Cos went on: "There was plenty of warning. There were increasingly large wildfires, most notably in the Western United States. Longer and more intense tropical storms devastated coastlines all over the world. And then, the draughts, downpours, and ice melts started to kill marine ecosystems and raise sea levels. It happened because of the proliferation of carbon dioxide, $CO_2$. While it is vital to all living creatures, too much or too little means death to all. Fortunately, my family watched the signs.

"My family and others took heed," Cos continued. "They left just days before. The Earth became only rock, pebbles and sand orbiting in space with the other stars. But here you are, with your pond and berries! I believe you are the only survivor!"

"Why weren't we warned?" I exclaimed as though in my asking something could have been changed.

"Yes," he said, "There were plenty of signs, but not many people listened. The first large jump in $CO_2$ – more than the world could reabsorb – happened during the Industrial Revolution in the last century.

"Yet many nations around the Earth turned a blind eye to the $CO_2$ overload. Change was particularly difficult because people were afraid it would lead to more layoffs and fewer profits. But my family and others saw the dire consequences of too little action. They kept looking for the world's willingness to adjust to the reality of $CO_2$ imbalance and finally gave up.

"My parents and others frantically searched for a place to go. They spent days in libraries, sought out knowledgeable professors and visited planetariums. From a distance, someone spotted a far-off planet, green, with seemingly nothing to upset the natural balance of carbon dioxide. The group studied space travel which was still in its infancy. They weighed the risks of staying against the risks of going. They decided staying was sure death and going was dangerous but with some hope. After much thought and many prayers, they moved out. Their destination was the planet Aura where my family and others landed 26 years ago."

"My parents were part of the waves of hundreds of people who left on spaceships to a planet that appeared livable. In many ways it resembled what Earth once was, with plenty of oxygen, water, and natural growth. Those boarding their flight knew they were taking the paramount gamble of their lives," he said. "Nothing was certain, but the fright of staying weighed heavier than the risk of leaving.

"On Aura, they found vast forests, fertile fields, running creeks and large, fresh-water lakes filled with fish. The temperatures are moderate, the air is clean and clear. Each morning it is as if the planet had been scrubbed clean leaving a blanket of moisture. Immediately, they formed a clean-energy society with a democratic government and created an educational system that is superior. It all happened quickly. The new population was motivated."

"We speak largely English with a number of other languages," Cos went on. "The majority of us are from English speaking societies but language differences include French, Chinese, Korean, Spanish, Russian, Hebrew, Arabic, Swahili, and German. They have blended together over the years. My dad had been an engineering professor while mom taught ancient history. It is academics like them who are responsible for Aura's leading-edge knowledge stored in our computers, books and memories.

"All our agriculture is planet-grown (of course; where else?), and everything manufactured is locally sold since we have no foreigners with whom we can trade. All the work in the fields and orchards is accomplished by computer-operated machinery developed in our University engineering laboratories."

"Aura University is all-important. From it flows the initiatives in all fields: engineering, agriculture, medicine, art, history, languages, economics, chemistry, philosophy, theater, psychology, and the religions of the world," he said.

"We have no foreign enemies. There is no one outside the planet to fight. So, we have no army. Everyone understands the need for some police and a few judges to maintain law and order. But generally, our citizens are peaceful and happy. Much of that can be credited to a planet-wide voluntary mentoring program."

He continued, "Our mission here on Earth will return in time for our annual gala that overflows with music and cheer. It celebrates the advances made in our society this past year. Especially of high interest at this festival will be stories of this trip to Earth. The public already knows much about our mission here. Reports of our work have been the daily news back home. But we, the team, will be on stage at the festival for hours answering questions about this mission.

"Also high on the interest list will be the inaugural of the first ten miles of the vacuum-tube system that will eventually transport people and cargo to the furthest reaches in Aura. We have been working on this for years. Further, honored will be time-saving inventions. This year's prize winners include home-making advances such as the one-minute bedding changer and the whole-house dust extinguisher taking three to ten minutes depending upon the size of the house.

"Unhappiness? When it happens, there is our mentoring program. As we grow as a nation, it may become more difficult, but I hope not," he said.

We stood in silence.

Finally, he said, "Come on, I will hook us up to the cable and radio to be pulled up. We both are going to Aura."

"Oh no!" I protested. "No, no. I am fine here!"

"But you can't be here for the rest of your life," he said.

"I have grown comfortable. No more change! No more! I have peace. My bubbling spring is my soothing rhapsody. I cannot leave nor do I want to leave."

He protested, "I will not leave you. I owe it to you to get you out of here."

"Please understand, Captain." I felt t my muscles tightening. "My roots are here. This home is who I am. If I turn my back from it, I no longer will be me." My eyes turned moist, blinking. Tears flowed onto my beard which nearly touched my waist.

Suddenly, he grabbed me and lashed me to the cable.

"Stop!" I struggled to be free. "Stop!" I tried to fight him off as the cable slowly pulled both of us upward.

# CHAPTER 2

## A HIDEOUS FLIGHT TO AURA

I lost control, sobbing hysterically, feeling everything was happening too fast.

When we reached the top of the canyon, I could make out four figures rushing forward to gather around us. Ahead was a huge grey spaceship, harbored horizontally. Two of Captain Cos's men, one on either side of me, forced me aboard and strapped me into a cushioned brown leather seat. As soon as they turned their backs and walked up the aisle, I unbuckled myself, ran down the aisle. Two of them grabbed me. One of them lifted my body and another my legs. I was no match for them. They carried me to my seat. While the two held me still, another came. Squeezed my upper arm and inserted the needle. I quickly became limp and my mood mellowed.

Captain Cos paid no attention to my attempted escape, obviously never doubting the outcome. He was busy talking into his microphone with someone on Aura about me. When he finished, he turned his attention across the aisle to me.

"Listen, you will never be able to return to Earth, even if you want to. You have to face reality and welcome your new life." Nerves kept me from normal breathing. I was trapped.

The spaceship had thick, brown leather padding on the floor, ceiling and walls, except for the windows which were round and clear. It was like being a prisoner in a big, brown box with no way out. I felt increasingly drowsy and was beginning to dose off when Captain Cos roughly shook my shoulder.

"I have arranged for your haircut and shave as soon as we land," he said. Then he called for two of his men to lift me to a standing position and to hold me upright as he measured my body for length and width in response to questions he got from Aura.

Whenever I awakened, I was served with a sparse portion of rice and berries and then was accompanied to the bathroom. They would not allow for the door to be shut. This became the routine for the next seven days though my food portions grew steadily. Each morning and evening I was forced to sip apple juice. Someone stood over me to make certain I drank every drop. The juice seemed to relax my mind and body. At first, I would be asleep within minutes. As the trip continued, my awake time increased. By the time of the last day of the of the flight came, the fruit-juice routine was history.

Having been so roughly treated thus far, I was terrified of what would happen next.

# CHAPTER 3

## ADJUSTING TO THE IDYLIC LIFE ON AURA

Upon our arrival, a man talked with Captain Cos and then he and the guards took me to an empty room with only a plain wooden table and chairs. I watched as each of my treasured items – my books, backpack, my note from my mother – all were carefully placed in a metal box with a lock and key.

Then, Cos and another man stripped off my clothes. A barber arrived and gave me a short haircut and clean shave. Two doctors checked my skin, examined my body, took samples of blood, urine, measured my eye movement, and gauged the strength of my arms and legs.

A driver with a military brown-painted car took the Captain and me to a large hospital. Captain Cos said he would be sleeping in the adjoining room for the next several days and that nurses would be outside my door 24 hours a day.

In the morning, 14 sets of clothes, 18 pieces of underwear, two sets of shoes, a coat, a jacket and a cap arrived. My meals were small but delicious: beef, green vegetables, potatoes and fruit. Each day, however, the amount grew. In a week, I was eating steak dinners.

After several days, Captain Cos offered to show me around. The outside air was warm, crisp and clean. There are flowers in window boxes, along public walkways, and in front of public buildings. "There is not a smokestack on the planet," he said. He pointed out that all automobiles, tractors and heavy building equipment were battery operated and manufactured by one company which was founded and operated by settlers from Earth who had worked for Ford, John Deere and CASE in the United States. Available for sale were trucks that looked like Expeditions, Silverados and Jeeps. Green farm machinery and yellow heavy-duty equipment rolled off assembly lines.

"We use almost no paper or plastic. Our manufacturing, packaging and transactions are digital, thanks to eight families from Silicon Valley and two from Tsukuba, Japan," he said. "There are not many shops because most purchases are transacted by tablets and delivered from warehouses by drones. Most homes have a drone box that will signal to the owner that the delivery has arrived as well if it includes perishable groceries. The boxes are unlocked and then relocked be delivering drone and is capable of handling large deliveries. There is never a chance of a drone collision. Sensors automatically force detours then return the drones to their original routes. Restaurants, entertainment parks and sporting events are abundant, and we have sunbathing at beaches and hiking in the mountains."

After two weeks, I was moved to an apartment with a living room, bedroom, small kitchen and bath. Someone had kindly placed a large basket of fruit on the dresser. Just outside my door, in the hall, an attendant sat ready to respond 24 hours a day to me and the guests in other apartments.

Captain Cos remarked that if I could understand only one dimension of this planet, he would choose Aura's government-funded, voluntary mentoring program. He believes that is what makes Aura's society distinctively magnificent.

"Its mission is to assist in resolving upsetting occurrences before they become problematic and causing hurt to fester into hatred. It functions to help citizens achieve peaceful, inventive, spiritual, artful and prosperous lives. This initiative has been in place Aura for years," he said.

"Our citizens, refugees from Earth, recalled how on Earth, humanity was clumped into snarling tribes of nations, races, religions, political parties and social groups warring against one another: killing, squeezing, tricking, mocking, embarrassing, threatening and cheating.

"On Aura, they worked to prevent such clashes before they could devolve into hostility. A solution came from Colonel Hugh Wise, a man who on Earth had been in law enforcement in the small town of Fenton, Michigan in the United States. While he and his fellow officers struggled to bring order to Earth, crime continued to grow in ferocity.

In gatherings around Aura, this Colonel was quite vocal, insisting that animosities must be quelled before they could intensify. His approach to accomplish this: a voluntary nationwide free mentoring service directed by therapists and psychiatrists and carried out by citizens.

Many thought the mentoring plan was weak but had no stronger alternative. Since the Colonel was so cocksure it would succeed, many thought it deserved a try. And if it did not work, Aura would try something else.

I wanted to get to know more about this mentoring program, so Captain Cos took me to meet the 67-year-old Colonel Wise. I found him to be friendly, quick witted, tall, weathered face and a chiseled jawline. With his wife, Helaine, their children and their friends' families, they had boldly fled Earth more than a quarter-century earlier.

Coronel Wise's office had a sliding glass wall that rolls open to a patio surrounded by a garden of yellow, white and red roses. We sat down to a frosty pitcher of mixed fruit juices, rum, and two chilled glasses. I asked the him about his planet-wide mentoring program.

"It is about the future of Aura," he said. "We take pride that we may be on the verge of inventing a lasting utopia. Yet, after a few years, we began to see small cracks in what we thought was perfection.

"At this point," he said, "our problems are small, but as we grow, many kinds of troubles are likely to seep into our society unless we identify and attack the shortcomings. How can we sustain the beautiful magic we have? We believe our mentoring and mentee program is the answer. We *think* it is the answer."

He explained, "The mentees choose from a list of available mentors. At any time, the relationship can be mutually terminated. It does not work well unless there are exit doors available to both. The mentor's job is to listen carefully to the mentee," he said.

"First, the individual seeking guidance describes the problem uninterrupted. Eventually, the mentor offers suggestions, if appropriate. Mentors are schooled to recognize deeper-sown issues," the Colonel explained. "When faced with a more profound situation, the mentor can offer the mentee help from a more deeply qualified specialist such as a psychologist, a lawyer or a social worker. In those cases, the mentor usually continues as an advisor to the mentee as he or she interacts with the specialist. Information about the mentee is not allowed to be shared without the mentee's consent, except in dangerous circumstances.

"Mentors learn the people or situations that disturb their mentee's peace and happiness. And they look deeper to understand why. Most of the time, the solutions become clear quickly," he said.

"Aura's mentoring program is immensely popular and growing. Even the most emotionally healthy people are using it regularly, sometimes if for nothing else but for an objective opinion on a matter. Currently, 38% of the teenage and adult population are taking advantage of the program and that figure is projected to climb to 72% within the next eight years."

I asked if he could describe several typical successes and challenges.

"Here are three examples of challenges we face," Colonel Wise said. "In one, a wife fell in love with her mentor and told her husband she wanted a divorce to marry the mentor. This happens from time to time when a client becomes so appreciative of a mentor's help that love is born. What I did was to assign a second mentor to counsel both husband and wife. The husband came in for several sessions and he discovered he needed to listen and pay more attention to her. He really loved her, but she was frustrated by the lack of his attention. She really did not fall in love with her mentor. She fell in love with the attention she was getting from the mentor.

"In a different case, a man in his mid-50s, quite bright, strong and dashing with a winning way, would at first rush to do favors no one thought were needed. Then he would fail in all his promises, become a constant source of untruths, make more promises and not keep one of them, while artfully dodging all questions about them. Then after months, he would return to do favors, lie about them and then renege. His workplace boss encouraged him to enter the program. Our arbitrator worked with him weekly for months, but with no success. We suggested he should see a psychologist. He refused. Then see a psychiatrist. He refused. He was found to be mentally ill, but we remained unable to reach him. Ultimately we had no recourse but to close the case.

"Finally, there was the case of a 15-year-old girl with a loud gibble-gabble voice and tight short skirts, who sashayed through the halls of her high school. She wondered why she was outcast by other students. A teacher recommended her to the program, thinking we may be in a good position to help her. We matched her with one of our youngest female mentors and the case was resolved in a very short order of time. Our 15-year-old wasn't aware of the tone of her voice and her choice of clothes. She couldn't see how she was being perceived. That mentor has become her go-to person whenever she has a problem of any sort.

"We always are thinking of how we might better serve seriously troubled mentees. They tend to relapse and drift from their paths to success. We are experimenting with ways for a mentor to alert a mentee when he or she starts going off course from the desired goals.

"We know that certain breeds of dogs have an excellent sense of routine and they are quite teachable. The concept can be likened to the seeing-eye dog program. We are trying to build a help system using the seeing-eye model where the mentor would recognize approaching trouble and whimper an alert. This study is in an early stage," Colonel Wise said.

"We are becoming a lucrative society. We have the financial strength that allows us to explore initiatives that serve our citizens." he said. "As a nation, we have no enemies. We are the only population on this planet, and we know of no enemies on others. So, we do not need a defense department. On Earth, where most of us came from, defense could be roughly one-third of a nation's budget.

"So, we have more money for services that help our citizens. "I and many others believe the wisest investment we can make is in keeping our citizens' hearts and hearts untroubled. That will allow for the magic of Aura to continue."

I had no more questions. We stood. I thanked him. As he walked to the corridor, he was politely chatty, during which he said: "We are pleased that you are going to be one of us. Would you agree to having a mentor from our program to assist your orientation into your new planet?"

"Of course," I said. "This would be very smart and appreciated."

Within several days the Captain introduced to my new mentor, a woman named Susan Darl. She had a big smile, friendly voice and seemed intelligent and principled. We immediately became fast friends. Laughter with her was a delight. We had long discussions about what occupation I should pursue. I suggested farming, so she arranged for me to spend a week working on a produce farm. I spent another week interning in a bank, and then as a teacher's assistant, and still another as a restaurant waiter's assistant. After more thought, I mentioned space travel. "I have some experience as a passenger," I said in a jocular way.

Susan knew that Aura University offered studies in rocket science and operated a spaceship technology and manufacturing facility. She lauded Aura's program and said if it was not exceptional, the mission to Earth would never have happened. A few Aura families have their own spaceships parked on their backyard launching pads for recreational use. "That shows the breath of interest stimulated by the program," she said.

She promised that she would make some calls and get back to me.

A day later she phoned. "A four-day flight into outer space is leaving in tomorrow. Major Dan Hanshaw, one of our top rocketeers, will be in command. Colonel Wise and Captain Cos both believe this is an important opportunity for our Earth resident. Do you want to go? They need to know now."

"No question," I said. "YES!"

I told Susan as she drove me to Aura University's spaceship facility how much I appreciated what she had done for me. She asked if I felt relief being away from Earth and in a safe place. At first, I did not answer. I thought about saying "yes" to be done with it. No. I needed to be truthful with myself and with my mentor.

"Not really," I said. "Earth is where life and love and traditions were passed down to me. What has become me is from my inherited family values and traditions. I feel I need to return to my home, Earth, if only temporarily, or remain unsettled."

"Well," she said, "that is impossible, as sadly, Earth has become desolate and uninhabitable. Its atmosphere is ruined, its soil destroyed. Your tiny stream of water which sustained you is a rarity on this otherwise dead planet."

I nodded. "I suppose so."

We had arrived at the Aura University space travel facility. I was taken to meet Major Hanshaw, who was short and muscular, with dark hair and of the type who speaks only when he has something to say. Then, the attendants fitted me into a space suit. I was given a daylong crash course of space travel passenger protocol, which primarily entailed remaining still and silent in my seat for the majority of the trip and allowing Major Hanshaw to manage the flight controls.

I was shown to a relatively small silver-colored craft with three deep grey seats in a row. First was the pilot's, the second one behind him where I was to be and the third behind me was to remain vacant for this test flight. The walls were covered with digital screens and controls.

For takeoff, I was told, the seats would be horizontal but would tilt upright as soon as we rise outside of gravitational pull. I strapped in, shut my eyes, and waited. Hours later, with Major Hanshaw in charge, the engines roared and we catapulted forward.

Flung back in my seat hurtling through the air, I loved it.

I watched in astonishment from my seat as this flawless wonder unfolded before my eyes. However, that soon changed. After hours of motion, suddenly the digital screens went blank. Both sending and receiving communications suddenly grew silent. The Major twisted in his seat as he checked gauges in the panels on each side in front of him and on the ceiling of the cockpit. Was I imagining it, or were the directional and velocity control of the ship lost? All my blood seemed to leave my body. We were barreling nowhere with no choices.

# CHAPTER 4

## SPEEDING TO DEATH IN OUTER SPACE

Exhausted! Sleepless! Terrified! In an icy sweat, body trembling. Breathing with great difficulty even with an oxygen mask. I knew that we were out of control in outer space.

I tried to calm myself by thinking of pleasant memories of life once lived. I thought of my mom. I remembered her note, of course, and wondered about it as it lay in the locked metal box in Aura. I remembered my dad, my sister, my pug dog Happihour, and my best friend since we were babies, Coolade. I thought about the home run I hit to win a little league baseball game. I wondered if there is any semblance of the Ohio River left on Earth where, as a family, we boated on hot Sundays. I tried to find reasons to be grateful for surviving. Hadn't I had enough of life? Why didn't I die along with everyone else?

After three days in space, there was suddenly a flicker of light on the video screens, causing distant hope. Major Hanshaw tirelessly attempted to make contact. Then, nothing. All quiet for another day. Suddenly, we heard a female voice faintly. She seemed to be reading a long list of words, pausing between each. Was it languages she was listing? Then she said, "English." Her enunciation was near perfect.

"Yes, yes!" Major Hanshaw shouted. "English!"

Soon after, the voice came in over the space ship's communication system, speaking English. She said if we continued the course we were traveling, we would be entering the airspace of the planet Idel. "Our lethal rocket system will connect with your ship and destroy it if you do not reverse your direction immediately," the voice said.

"Not possible," Major Hanshaw shouted. "We come with no ill will from the planet Aura. We were on an experimental test flight and all systems have failed. We cannot cause harm. We have no weapons onboard, only the two of us."

The voice stated we needed to verify the truth of that.

"We have been struggling to contact Aura," the Major said, and asked if there was a way she could relay our situation to Aura or assist in getting a distress message about us to anyone.

The woman over the airwaves replied that Idel had heard no sounds from space except for more than two decades ago, when they picked up on talking they believed to be from the planet Earth.

She stressed that our safety was totally up to us. The decision to attack already had been made by Idel's Senate. "We will take no chances since the lives of our citizenry may be at stake," the voice said. She informed us they were prepared to shoot us out of the sky if we entered their airspace.

"How long will it be before you shoot?" asked Major Hanshaw, urgently.

"It is whatever the full Senate determines," the woman said.

Which meant that any moment, we could be blown to pieces. One minute came and went and then another. Silence. What felt like days later, the woman who spoke English back and regained contact with our ship. She and a panel of 12 questioned us about Aura, Earth, our jobs, our educations, our experiences, our religions, our birth places, our parents, our family lives, our memberships, our hobbies. None of them sounded friendly. The stress was extreme. We expected, any moment, to die.

# CHAPTER 5

## A CLOUD OF NERVES

We are alive. Radar pulses pulled us to a landing in a desolate, dusty and dark field on the planet Idel. It was humid and the air felt stale and heavy. Tanks rumbled into a circle around us. An armored truck approached. As we climbed from the spaceship, three soldiers appeared with weapons raised. What appeared to be their commander stepped forth and motioned to another soldier to strip off our flight suits. Our arms were bound behind our backs. Then our ankles were tied in such a way that we could shuffle only inches at a time.

We were driven several miles to a one-story, concrete building consisting only of one dirty-grey room with a white toilet and sink and two unpainted wooden chairs. The Commander directed the Major and me to sit. I looked around. The room had only two small windows with bars.

We were untied and a crucial but polite language skirmish began. It was apparent the Major was being asked to describe our situation.

He used body language as well as growls and whimpers to try to make his points. After an hour, he had made only limited headway. The Commander and his soldiers departed, locking the door behind them.

But what we believed was that Idel's scientists had created an advanced listening technology, though we were not certain about this because, in the conversation with the Commander, we made assumptions to bridge our ideas and his. The woman who had spoken English to us through the spacecraft's communication system had said that Idel had, for years, occasionally heard noises from Earth. Therefore, the language spoken on Idel is a mishmash of sounds from Earth. Devotees of this practice had woven sound patchworks believed to be a language.

This language bridging initiative, we later learned, was carried out by the same woman who had spoken English to us while we were in space. She had done much to turn around the Senate's thinking which eventually allowed us to land on planet Idel.

Soon a soldier arrived with two thin mattresses, some clothing, slippers, blankets and pillows. A dim night-light was activated, somehow, and we slept.

The next morning a soldier brought us a wooden tray of nuts and fruits, and a pot of coffee with two metal cups. In the early afternoon, we were brought a larger tray of nuts and fruits and a pitcher of fruit juices, and again a still larger tray as it grew dark.

With each appearance, we tried to learn our destiny. Each time, we could discern nothing. Everyone we saw had rusty, blond skin.

On the fifth day, two soldiers came in a truck to take us to a government building in the city. During the ride, I marveled at both the similarities well as the dissimilarities between Aura and Idel. The planet Aura is like Earth in the way it had been constructed. Architecture, cars, highways are akin. Of course, the primary reason is that Aura settlers brought their Earth ways with them. Idel's building materials resembled those of both Earth and Aura. Bricks, glass and concrete were prevalent. I found this remarkable, given that it is totally outside the influence of the other two planets. They must have experimented and arrived at similar conclusions.

Idel also had cars and trucks but the ones here had either three or six wheels. By the smell of black exhaust fumes, it is obvious the vehicles are fueled by oil. And there is plenty of coal burning. The Major and I both immediately noted the pollution and the stench of the air.

What was notably different were the shapes. This truck I was riding in was oval rather than rectangular. The configurations of the brick and glass buildings along the way seemed to be placed at awkward angles, with unusual curves and incongruous juxtapositions.

We were taken into a building and ushered to a room with a polished oblong table and cushioned chairs where we were directed to sit. The soldiers sat behind us with their weapons. We waited quietly. The room had a sliding glass wall that opened onto a deck overlooking a rather poorly-cared-for garden with a fountain in its center spouting water several feet high. I was struck by the contrast.

Moments later, the door opened and walking briskly to greet us was a beautiful woman with large, friendly dark eyes, straight black hair and a gracious smile. "Hello. My name is Trussx," she said in a friendly tone of understandable English. We were both prepared to use sign language, but it quickly became obvious it was not needed.

"Very pleased to meet you," the Major said. In response I, as I had been doing for days, silently nodded in agreement.

She began by saying, "At first, most of my fellow Idel Senators were against allowing the two of you to land, as we feared for the safety of our citizenry. You may recall I told you as much when you were in the air. Yes, that was me communicating with you since I have been for years to catalog the galaxy's languages.

"A recording of your conversations on board your spacecraft was assessed using an algorithm designed by an assembly of psychologists, trial lawyers, employment directors and law-enforcement officers, all of whom form judgements about people partly from the manner of talk. We were able to confirm that what you said and the way you said it is honest and convincing.

"One more important point. Major, would you tell me about your level of experience in rocket design?"

Major Hanshaw talked about his classroom education, his on-the-job training, and his years working his craft while at the same time teaching engine and rocket design at Aura University.

"Would you be willing to do the same for us here on Idel?" Trussx asked.

"I would be honored," Major Hanshaw replied.

She stood, shook our hands and officially welcomed us to planet Idel.

Then we all sat down again. "Please," she said, "Before you are shown your guest apartments, I would like to explain to you how I know English. For years, I have been trying to follow sounds from the galaxy," she said. "It was silent but for planet Earth, where I could pick up glimmers of communication that were occasionally heard but then no longer."

I interrupted. "Earth is where I was born! Fire engulfed the entire planet 26 years ago, making the planet no longer livable. It was an apocalypse."

She stared at me with eyes wide open, and then after a moment, continued: "I have been pursuing an interest in Earth since childhood. I now am a Senator and in a position that allows me and several other like-minded Senators to strike a deal. And that we did.

"And I must be honest," she continued. "The odds may still be against us. Most of the Senators and a few influential citizens they represent were vehemently opposed to allowing you to land here. However, you had no other options. Either land or continue to fly until you burned to death. We took that into consideration when making the decision.

"Here is what has been done: The Senate has given tentative approval if the outcome of this meeting with me is positive. So far, so good. Particularly, we look forward to Major Hanshaw sharing his knowledge of space travel with us. I will make certain to tell them, Major, that your response is 'I am honored.' Is that correct?"

"Absolutely!" he said.

"Know they will be most pleased when they learn this," Trussx replied. "New knowledge enables progress in many ways.

"Your apartments in this building will be your homes until you are able to settle yourselves on this planet. Major, I need to talk to my fellow Senators about you, but I believe they will want you to work through Idel University and lend your counsel to our space efforts."

Trussx told me that I would be working five days a week on government construction and maintenance crews, a different one each day.

"You will have jarring jobs. If you make positive impressions, it will help sell the idea of your becoming one of our citizens. However, we now fear for your safety particularly if you stay in your workplace communities overnight. Many of our citizens living outside the cities disagree with what we are doing, so we will see that you are transported safely to and from your workplaces. The people of Idel tend to be frightened of strangers, especially ones that drop from outer space." She smiled at that.

She went on to say, "I will be your government contact. You will be compensated for your work. When you have an issue, come to me.

"Oh, and one more thing. I will help the both of you get settled here. My husband and I want to welcome you in our home. We look forward to be learning about Aura and Earth from you."

We stood, thanked her, shook hands and she left. Major Hanshaw and I looked at each other, jaws agape, stunned at the sudden turn of events on Planet Idel.

A receptionist motioned for us to be seated in a reception area of a large office to wait for our transportation. I could not help but notice the styles of dress differing from those on Aura. Young women on Idel are bare from the waist up and wear tight skirts with large holes showing their bare buttocks. Young men's pants are tight, and they too have gaps showing their bare buttocks.

Older professionals wear more muted tones. Trussx, for example, wore a rust-colored dress that was form fitting from her neck to inches above her knees. Older men dressed casually and no one wore anything resembling a tie. I believed no one on this planet knew what a tie was, and if they did know, they probably would laugh.

# CHAPTER 6

## A ROCKY START

I had completed the first week of my work on the planet Idel and it is 5 p.m. I am in a meeting with Trussx, my ultimate supervisor, in her office which is in the same government building as the apartment she has arranged for me.

"I am sorry about the miscommunication," she said. "On days you work in the field, your driver is supposed to pick up a lunch pail for you from the cafeteria downstairs. I just learned that you missed receiving several of them. You went hungry on the first two days. I am so sorry. Have you received the last three?

"Oh yes, thank you."

"Were they adequate?

"Yes, thank you."

"Tell me about them."

"Yes. One included ham and beans mixed on a healthy amount of rice and another was a large bacon, lettuce and tomato sandwich on rye. Both included sugar cookies and fruit juice."

"And the third?" she asked.

"There was a mix-up on the first day."

"After the kitchen caught the mistake, they had the lunch delivered to you."

"Yes." I was trying to think how to get onto another topic.

"Did the missing one arrive?"

"Oh yes. It arrived," I said.

"Well, what did it consist of?"

There is silence as I tried to circumvent this topic and move on. But she would not have it.

"Why? What happened to it?

"The other workers divided it among themselves."

After a long pause, she asked, "And you sat hungry and watched?"

"No. They were sitting away from me. " I hoped she would stop. I needed no enemies on this strange planet. A misstep could mean my life.

She asks if I had experienced any other impoliteness in the in the field, at Idel University, or around the city.

I really did not want to get further into this conversation. However, it would be worse if I did not give a straight answer to her direct question. In the long run, I needed her to trust me.

"Yes," I responded, "Several times while walking on campus, students as well as faculty members coming the other way crossed the street as they approached, and then as soon as they were past me returned to my side of the street."

"How many times did this happen?"

"Four that I noticed."

"We have our work cut out for us, haven't we?"

"I can handle it," I said.

"No, you and I will handle it together," she replied.

# CHAPTER 7

## BLACK SMOKE AND BLIND MEN

Four weeks later, I am sitting for dinner at the home of Trussx and her husband, Hotten, discussing the robust industry on Idel which is beefy and bottom-line successful.

"Major Hanshaw could not join us tonight," Trussx said, "He is busy with students, spaceship builders and university faculty events; I seldom see him anymore." Then, after the three of us discussed what I have been through on Earth and up the present, I directed the focus onto Hotten. He spoke uninterrupted for five or so minutes. I learned his first job was in a factory working as a helper, meaning he had to go here then there to do this or that where an extra hand was needed. His father had been a plant foreman. His entire life had revolved around the manufacturing industry.

Hotten spoke with a swagger about Idel's industrialization. "It is the backbone of this flourishing society," he said. "The industry leaders of Idel are insightful and kind. One I know gives each employee a turkey for his or her winter holiday and delivers them personally to each employee's home. The delivery schedule is distributed so that each knows when he will arrive."

I smiled, marveling at how both Earth and Idel had arrived independently at the same bad idea.

"What other benefits are provided to the citizens of Idel?" I asked. "Health care?"

"There are company funded health clinics for on-the-job accidents."

Do employees ever gather to communicate with him?

"No need to gather. Each employee is free to speak for himself, having no fear of repercussion."

"You say himself. Ever herself?"

"Yes. Equal opportunity. Trussx would not have her position if there were not general acceptance."

Trussx added, "That has been happening only recently, and not as often as it should be."

I asked about the health of the environment on Idel, noting that my days with the work crew revealed the majority of industries were marked by smokestacks and plumes of thick, black smoke. Was it wrong to conclude that Idel possibly was on a frightful course to a catastrophic end, just like Earth?

Hotten answered for Trussx: "That is not a worry here. There is plenty of clean air so there is no danger. What happened on Earth will not happen here, ever."

I glanced over to Trussx, who avoided my eyes.

We closed the evening with friendly talk and laughs over sips of brandy.

At our next meeting, Trussx asked if I had spoken with anyone else on Idel about my experience with the $CO_2$ imbalance on Earth.

"Yes. I talked about it with one of my work gangs as well as some people at the university. I believe I owe it to humanity to describe the peril."

She said that this kind of talk would make my acceptance on Idel difficult. "Don't get me wrong. You are doing what you need to do. But change is hard. If your family, friends and neighbors think one way, it is challenging and often punishing to shift their thinking to another way.

"The majority of people on Idel think like Hotten," she continued. "They are fully comfortable just the way they are, and wary of anything that is different."

"I dropped into here from another world," I reminded her.

"Yes. That causes you to be feared and untrusted," was her response.

# CHAPTER 8

## TRUSSX HAS A DREAM

Trussx canceled six of our weekly meetings. Then, when we finally got together, she explained, "I did not want to meet until I had more information to share. We are facing an issue that needs to be hit with everything we've got. It may be pivotal to a dream that I know we share.

"Here is what I have been doing. I met with seven senators, each with strong constituencies. Some owe me favors. To others, I have promised favors.

"I then went to the president of the Senate, the president of the university and our attorney general. After thinking about Earth's annihilation due to an imbalance of $CO_2$, we agreed to initiate a massive alarm and explore ways to prevent that from happening to us. It also was agreed to investigate the possibility of space travel to planet Aura. After learning about the Earth's apocalypse, we recognize that Idel and Aura might someday need one another.

"As Senator in charge of the program, I have named you my full-time chief of staff. We need to repeatedly tell audiences your personal story. Tell them about Earth, Aura and Idel. You are the only person who can do so. Our current environmental conditions here on Idel somewhat match Earth's past environmental situation. It could happen to us. We must crusade to make certain it does not."

She looked at me as she continued. "You no longer will be on the work crew. Your new role is to work with me following a final vote of the Senate. There is no chance of the vote failing. It is politically assured. You will keep your apartment rent-free and your remuneration will be commensurate with the position you will hold," she told me.

"One more thing. Be ready for a fierce and unrelenting counterattack by conservatives at some point. And know that while we may win the first several rounds, we are going to have to work hard at the grass roots level if we are going to be successful. We need develop a powerful message for large and small assemblies across the planet."

I told her I am thrilled and impressed at her foresight and the degree of her aggressive accomplishments. "Congratulations! You can flood me with difficult assignments. Saving another planet from being destroyed is not to bad as a life's mission."

"I know that," she said. "I feel the same way. I should tell you about Hotten and me. He is firmly on one side and I am unwavering on the other. We have no children and we both realize our marriage is a stormy sea. However, we both are professional and we each have our own careers. I am just fearful they may collide. I look around on Idel and I know we need to prepare ourselves for brutal battle. I dread that it may be against Hotten.

"I want to campaign against smokestacks emitting too much $CO_2$. You will see what that does to Hotten. I have loved him and do not want to hurt him. He adores his work and friends, most of whom are in those polluting industries. On the other hand, this is the undertaking I feel I have been waiting for all my life. It is *that* important. I want us to clean up Idel, create a shuttle between Idel and Aura, share the best thinking from people from both planets and perhaps someday join with them as one interplanetary nation."

I couldn't believe the opportunities that were opening before me. Me, the silent passenger on the test flight with Major Hanshaw.

"Trussx," I told her, "I cannot be more thrilled. There is no more important purpose in my life than to support you in this most vital vision. Call me any hour of the day for work needing to be done."

"I already have planned to do that," she said. "To facilitate this working partnership, I will be moving into an apartment downtown, to have a physical location that will allow me to do my best and most efficient work. It is in the same government building in which you are housed, but on a different floor. And, I believe it is best for my marriage to not go come home each week night and clash with my husband on this issue."

# CHAPTER 9

---

## PREPPING FOR THE PUSH

As Trussx had predicted, full Senate approval of the Idel climate initiative was easily clinched. Prior to the voting, Trussx insisted that Professor Higrow be added full-time to our team. He was the distinguished professor of sciences at Idel University and our go-to expert on air, water, climate and pollution. His job was to make certain everything is factually based. He is an elderly man, short, stooped and greying with a bit of shuffle to his walk and a weak raspy voice. But his mind is strong.

The presentations introducing our initiative were to be introduced by Trussx. The first thing audiences would see was her broad smile that lit up the room with a positive glow. The words she would choose would be selected intelligently, her pronunciation clear, her voice friendly and strong. Overall, the presentation she would make would be masterfully logical and offered with exuberance.

Animation and graphics would be used to tell my story of being the only known survivor of the Earth meltdown. If there were questions of me, Trussx would do the translating.

Next, Professor Higrow would explain how the environmental calamity that happened to Earth could occur on Idel. To support his reasoning would be graphics outlining the sources and pollutants that could cause the deadly $CO_2$ imbalance.

As Trussx was to begin closing remarks, a brochure with our rationale would be distributed to attendees by members of our office staff. Trussx would invite questions and discussions. When the crowd would thin, she and the Professor would invite them forward for further discourse.

The next step was to create lucid and indisputable dissertation as our core message resulting from the professor's research. It would be the foundation from which all our messaging will grow and be widely communicated throughout Idel. A staff was to be hired to manage the campaign and extend it regionally.

The presentations to citizens did not mention anything about rocket travel; that would come only after we were able to confirm that missions to Aura are goofproof. Scientists specializing in the sending and receiving of soundwaves were exploring ways to initiate reliable communications between planets.

Professor Higrow's role on the team involved only research. The bulk of work was led by Trussx with my assistance, working six and sometimes seven days a week. Finally one would say, "Let's take a break," and we would head out for a walk together.

These relaxed moments sometimes veered from business to personal. Trussx wanted to learn more about what Earth meant to me since it was destroyed and I remained alone there all those years. I explained if I hadn't held onto those memories of what it had been, I would have died in the canyon. The memories amounted to the nourishment that kept me alive.

"I felt a responsibility to everyone I knew and to everyone I knew of," I said. "I owe it to all of those who ever lived on Earth. I am the last one standing and I am standing for all of them, proudly representing them after the evil fire storm. I am them."

"If you could return, would you?" she asked.

"In a minute. My job is incomplete," I replied.

"Did you ever think during those 26 years of what you might have been missing by being in the canyon? Your first dance? Your first kiss? Your first love? Married life? Children?"

"Of course," I said, "But if reality becomes impossible, like it was for me, those thoughts were limited to dreams."

"But it is no longer impossible, so why continue your dreams?" she asked.

Her question was met with silence.

"Okay," she said. "On to a related topic I know I should not ask, but since we are just business friends, and we should never discuss this again..."

(silence)

"What? Continue," I said.

"You arrived at the canyon at age 10 and you were totally alone there until you were 36. Right?"

"Are you going to ask about sex?"

"Yes," she said.

"Sex has been limited to my imagination," I replied.

"Male or female?"

"Female."

Her face flushed. She spun around and said, "I am sorry. It is late. I must go. My apologies."

# CHAPTER 10

## MAY I SLEEP HERE?

Trussx and I are gathering information that will become the bedrock of our presentations to the Idel public. We have met often with Professor Higrow to understand the data he has uncovered that supports of our message. Trussx has hired a young woman, Dockett, to fill the fourth paid position of the campaign. She will be recruiting volunteers and coordinating their work. Dockett was selected from 18 candidates because of her strong work history, excellent organizational skills and a sparkling winning way that should help in the enlistment of unpaid staffers. She is extroverted and bounced with enthusiasm.

The inaugural meeting was held four weeks later at the Midtown Hall of Assembly in a park surrounding the government buildings. On stage were dignitaries willing to lend their support to the planet-wide initiative, including the entire Senate. Trussx impelled 11

Senators to be seated on stage with her. An art studio was employed to design the brochure and a printing company to do the production work. As of today, Dockett has enrolled 27 helpers. The target we gave her was 25. Good indication.

A hired band played robust national music. Each Senator was introduced. Seven gave strong endorsements but the other four seemed impotent, which surprised and angered Trussx.

As we neared the end, the volunteers handed out brochures as the crowd was leaving. Some of the volunteers seem more interested socializing with their friends, leaving their areas of responsibility uncovered. Docket assures us that at future events she will make sure that does not happen. It was the first show and she was still feeling her way.

We are encouraged by the number of people who stayed after the scheduled question-and-answer time conducted by Trussx. Not knowing the language, I did not know how to interpret what they were saying.

Trussx was exhausted, but we needed to debrief. We picked up sandwiches and a bottle of whiskey at a deli-type store and headed over to my apartment. "I worry about those four Senators," said Trussx. "Did they seem cautious to you? I wonder if that means trouble.

"I could ask Hotten," she said. There was a pause, then she said, "Oh no, I can't."

It had been a tense past few days. I was in a chair, she on the sofa. We continued talking at a declining pace.

"I was thrilled by the crowd. Dockett and her volunteers really shook the trees to encourage attendance," she says. I agree.

Trussx circled back to talk about the four Senators, and then asked, "May I lie down for a moment? I am exhausted."

She began a sentence, but began dozing off, stirred awake, continued talking, and then dozed again. She murmured, "Do you think Higrow's research is solid?"

"I do."

"What about his presentation?

"It seemed good, me knowing the content but not the language."

She closed her eyes and breathed deeply, then shook herself awake and continued her analysis of everything that had occurred.

I asked, "Would you like me to see you to your apartment?"

Her eyes open, and she stares silently at the ceiling.

"No," she said. "May I sleep here?

"Yes," I whispered as I quietly walked away. "Good job today."

# CHAPTER 11

## UP, UP AND AWAY

The following day, back in the office, Trussx and I continued our discussion of the night before.

"I fear we are going to have difficulty getting through to some people," she said. "Those four Senators are smart. They should be energetically embracing this, but they are not. I can tell. They are only lukewarm. Can industry interests have gotten to them this quickly? They couldn't organize that fast.

"Last night," she continued, "I awakened worrying about skeptics. How many? I do not know. Dark clouds could form in the heads of any percentage without our knowing it. If we could know what is troubling them, we could address their concerns with facts. But we cannot do that until we know they are thinking. As it is, we are flying blind."

63

We both were quiet in thought.

I said, "We need someone who can study the voting landscape, talk to key people in all walks of life in personal one-on-one conversations, group discussions and surveys. I do not know about Idel, but on Aura, there are consultants that do just that."

"There are undesignated funds still in our budget," she said. "I will phone several friends for names of consultants to learn from them what they can do.

That afternoon, Trussx, Professor Higrow and I gave the first of what would become many presentations. It was held in a middle-class neighborhood. No band this time. No dignitaries. Just the three of us. There seemed to be interest in what we have to say. Some in the audience were serious, some appeared neutral, but too many wary.

The next day we headed over to the Idel University stage. The questions came flying. As an audience of academics, they dug into all aspects of the issue and the questioning lasted for hours. They saw the danger. It helped that Professor Higrow was there; they all knew him, which added credibility.

Next, in a wealthy neighborhood, there were many cynics. They believe life was too good to chance rocking the boat. Then at another group in a small village in the countryside, residents were leery. Trussx and I agreed they would feel that way about anything that is new. What met their comfort level was anything that has worked well already. Finally, in an industrial town, the audience shouted us down. "It will kill our jobs!" was their unified cry.

I leaned over to Trussx and said, "This is going to be a long road."

Two weeks later, we found out how long that road would be. Seemingly everywhere, through every channel, to every citizen, was the message,

FIGHT TO KEEP YOUR JOBS. KEEP IDEL THE WAY IT IS.

The statement that followed assured jobs would be lost, and the economy would sink into a deep depression, if the nation shifted to clean energy. Listed as dissidents of our campaign were 25 top manufacturing and business CEOs. At the top of the list was Hotten's name.

I tried, unsuccessfully, to reach Trussx by phone. There was no answer, which was odd. She was not at the office nor did she answer her cell or apartment phone. I knew that Hotten's involvement, though not surprising, must have been a major blow.

Then the phone rang. It was Major Hanshaw.

"We need to meet," he said with a seriousness in his voice. Within five minutes he was at my apartment.

"For the last three weeks here on Idel, I have been conversing day and night with Aura. The inter-planetary communications infrastructure here is outstanding – far advanced to that of Aura – and my team and I had only to make minor adjustments to be able to connect with Aura. In addition, the linguistics talent here is fantastic, far more advanced than Aura's. After working to learn and then improve their systems, and then to test them, we now believe enough progress has been made to deem interplanetary communications possible. Who knows what else is out there?

"This is stunning," Major Hanshaw continued. "The first person who should know about this is Trussx. She originated the push to make this happen and as a Senator wields tremendous control over the budget.

"My Commander believes she should know before anyone else, but I have failed to reach her.

"Also, Aura wants a delegation from Idel to visit. They would like this to happen as soon as possible to encourage public enthusiasm for their space effort, which is another part of Trussx's mission. They are envisioning Idel and Aura as having a trade agreement leading toward more sharing of technology and developing interplanetary travel.

"My commander needs to reach Trussx. Can you speak with her? We want to support Aura's wish to move fast, so they can surprise their population with a startling jump start."

"You need to know," Major Hanshaw said, "Every component of our Aura spaceship has been tested meticulously on the ground and in space. Passenger-friendly fixtures have been added."

I jump to my feet. "I'll go now and see if I can find her. I'll be in touch."

I think about what a triumph this is for both planets, a victory to be celebrated for a thousand years. Further, it will have ramifications for the campaign, possibly positive, possibility negative.

# CHAPTER 12

## BOMBSHELL

My first thought is Trussx. Is she with Hotten? Should I phone him to see if Trussx is there? I'll do that only as a last resort.

I pounded on her apartment door. "Trussx, it is me." I pounded again. No answer. Once more, still no answer. Then I hear a voice a barely audible voice say, "Go up to your apartment and I will be there in 10 minutes."

As I open the door to let her in, I see her eyes are red and puffy. "I met up with my husband last night. This is too much. A bit of business for him is more important than ... I guess we are both guilty of that. Okay, tell me what's so important."

I repeated everything Major Hanshaw told me. I said I could help by laying out the issues one by one for discussion.

"Please," she said.

I said, "You should not go on the trip to Aura. You are the face of the Idel campaign. If you go away, the opposition could play on the thought that change is a danger and you already are causing it. On the other hand, your being on the trip could give us victory because Idel will be proud of our achievements and many may come to our side.

"And further, we do not have a good read on what percentage of the Idel population is with them, and what percentage is with us. If we are not the majority, say only 45%, it will easier for our opposition to defeat us. It is only natural for undecided voters to vote what is popular."

"Yes," she said. "I will stay here and campaign."

"Well, who will go on the trip to Aura?" I asked.

She sat thinking for a while. "It's you. You go to Aura."

"Well, I would be in a good position to connect with people I already know and tell them about what interplanetary travel could become. I feel excited to return but hesitant at the same time."

Trussx said she wanted to think about this, and got up to leave.

Two hours later, my phone rings. She said, "Let's take a walk." We meet in the lobby and find a park bench.

# CHAPTER 13

## THE RETURN

She led off with: "So much is happening at once." I nodded in agreement.

Then she questioned again: "Are you really the one to go to Aura with the Major?"

"To be honest, I do believe it should be me. When I first landed on Aura with Captain Cos, I was looked upon as a startling novelty, a man from another world, which I truly was. But since I was brought there by the Captain, I was generally accepted because people knew and trusted him. I was introduced to the thought leaders and became friends with many of them. Cos opened the door allowing me to enter with comfort. Someone who did not have a previous connection would not have that advantage."

"Further," I said, "my place in day-to-day presentations is not essential to the campaign. Since I am not able to speak, someone other than me must tell my story. If I am not there, little or no value would be lost."

She looked away for a minute, and then said, "You are from another place. A stranger. An intruder. I understand. That somewhat clouds the reception people give you. That should not be the case, but it does," she said. "I have noticed people in the same occupations tend to dress alike. Not always, but generally it is true. People in the same neighborhood tend to dress alike. Generally, people feel more comfortable resembling the crowd rather than being the exception.

"You are from one planet and I am from another."

I asked, "Is that a drawback with us?"

"No, because I immediately recognized familiar brain waves that I liked," she said.

"Then," I say, "The best way to find a connection with a person is to dig deeper than what is found on their surface."

"Yes," she said. "I believe we both should keep this conversation in mind as we will be making so many decisions with so many types of people on both Aura and Idel. It will take vigilance.

"I will call Hanshaw's Commander to tell him it will be you making the flight," she continued. "It should remain top secret until the planning is fully completed. We do not want Hotten to seize on a small piece of it and publicly throw it at us. That is the way wars are lost."

She does not move. Seems preoccupied. I just sit and wait. Finally, she says, "Hotten is livid."

"Why?'

"He is seething about you and me."

"What have we done?"

"I phoned him last night. He wanted to talk and came over to my place. Bad quickly became worse. It was a two-hour fight. Horrible!"

"How did it end?"

"Ugly! We agreed to an official separation now, and, in time, cut ties completely. Our marriage is over."

Then she said, "He thinks there is something between you and me, something more than a business relationship. I hate to think it but the way he talked I sensed his group may play dirty and use you and me and our business relationship to fan hate to benefit their campaign. "Trussx, he will claim, has a person from another planet whispering into her ear."

Silence.

"This may be too personal of a question," I said. "The two of you seem so different in so many ways. What drew the two of you together? How did you meet?"

"His father and my dad worked together at Creamex Manufacturing. Dad was an electrician and Hotten's father Geeze was the plant foreman. Dad respected the position Geeze had attained and his constant fountain of jokes and pranks. Dad kept pushing Hotten and me together for as long as I can remember. "

"And your mom?"

"She was a school teacher and reserved. She always thought both Hotten and his father were blowhards. No question, she did not like them. She always said I could be whoever I wanted to be because I was talented in many ways. She thought I should take my time and meet many more people before settling down.

"Both Hotten and I were interested in politics," she continued. "Always have been. We became active in the conservative party. That shared interest helped lure me into marrying him. I liked his politics, jokes and upbeat manner. And they are the reason for where he is today. He makes the world jolly for his rich industrial clients."

"But you?" I said. "You are not a strong conservative."

"There are degrees of conservatism," she says. "I am not a conservative when it comes to caring for all of the sick and having educational opportunities open to all. I have more of a chance of accomplishing these goals by staying within the party. My voice is stronger in the house than it would be yelling from the outside."

"And your mother?"

"She is a conservative but in the closet, she is rather liberal," she said.

"I have never felt a separation between us, because I am really quite liberal," I said.

"That is true. I always felt that way."

Two days later, I met Major Hanshaw at the launch pad. I was amazed that the two of us had been on Idel already for 18 months, and now the two of us were off again, me as his passenger, about to return to Aura. With us was the leader of the Idel Senate, the Honorable Seeohehaw, who was representing the government of Idel and one of Trussx's top supporters.

Now rising in the spaceship, I got a good look at Planet Idel. I can clearly identify the industrial areas by the black smoke rising from them.

# CHAPTER 14

---

## SPACECRAFT: ELEGANT, SMOOTH AND FAST

Major Hanshaw and I were traveling in the same spaceship that we arrived in. I cannot believe how much renovation has been accomplished.

When we reached a point in travel where the craft turned from vertical to horizontal, it was possible to get up and move about.

The major said this return flight would last just two days, much faster than our trip from Aura to Idel.

"What!" I said. "You are joking."

"No," he said. "There was a brilliant engineering group in Idel that made many adaptations to spaceship to cut the flying time in half. This was necessary if shuttle between the two planets were ever to become a reality.

Stunned, I asked, "Does Trussx know this?"

"She has been so busy and has not been getting reports unless it is urgent," Major Hanshaw said.

"It may not have been urgent, but it certainly is now."

Seeohehaw also was surprised but expressed confidence in any project under Trussx's leadership.

Late the next day, Major Hanshaw began preparing to land. Aura came into view. Hanshaw scanned the ship's magnifying lens as we got closer.

"What is growing in that in the large field over there?" I asked

"Looks like a wind turbine farm," he said.

It was a smooth landing. Hundreds met us. Captain Cos rushed up and embraced me. Immediately behind him was Susan Darl, who had been my insightful mentor. With her was her husband Don. I often had dinner at their lovely home. Next up to greet me was Coronel Wise.

The Major and I were the honored guests at a luncheon reception they had arranged to welcome us. There were a few speeches of welcome. They had scheduled nothing for us for the afternoon and evening believing we would want to relax after the trip.

I phoned Trussx. She could hardly get out her words.

# CHAPTER 15

---

## TRUSSX'S PAIN

Trussx was sobbing as she read to me the words of a message that had been widely distributed.

"'Planet Aura has secretly embedded a man on Idel,'" she read. "'He has been living in the same building as Senator Trussx. This is a pre-invasion strategy of Aura. He is whispering in Trussx's ear, to rob us of our jobs, our land and our freedom.'

"The headline reads: 'URGENT WARNING OF ATTACK!' It is endorsed by 25 top manufacturing organizations and CEOs. Pictured is a photograph of you and me, laughing as we are coming down some steps," she said, her anguish palpable.

My first thought was how Trussx must feel, grieving a marriage that has turned to hate.

I did not want to acknowledge my shock.

"This is what ignites hateful people," I said.

And, then, now shouting: "You need immediate and constant protection from bodily harm."

"Yes. The government is on it," she said. "I did not have to ask. Soon after the first messages appeared, I was surrounded by guards. One stands 24 hours a day outside my door. I am never alone. I am so grateful," she said. "I have heard from all seven of the Senators on our side. They are shocked by this and stand firmly with me."

I told her "Such a gutter message is not worth a reply. Enough reasonable people will see this for what this is. We need to act quickly before their slander metastasizes. Here is what I think should be done:

"Loudly trumpet the accomplishment of the voice communications established between Idel and Aura. It is an incredible reality and that reality will last forever. The two planets can now communicate with one another in real time.

"Using the new communications setup between the two planets, we should push for live forums with groups of similar nature from Idel and Aura, learning each other's shared joys and concerns.

"Trussx, you should serve as the translator of those broadcasts. You know both languages, but more important, you would be the best in understanding the true nurture of the dialogue. This will lead to the opening of minds, and increased understanding.

"We need to recruit groups of like interests on both planets to talk to one another: teachers talking with teachers, mothers with mothers, CEOs with CEOs, farmers with farmers, children with children, factory workers with factory workers, and so on. Any discussions that could lead to political grandstanding should be avoided.

"My thought is for me to stay to push from here."

After a moment of silence, Trussx spoke. "Allow me to think about it overnight," she said.

"Will do."

The first thing the following morning she called to say, "Let's do it."

"When are you making the announcement about the opening of communications between the two planets?"

"Today," she said

"Can you include this intra-planet dialogue program into that announcement?" I asked.

"Yes."

I tell her, "I already had scheduled lunch with Colonel Wise. I will ask for his help with enrolling groups on Aura. This is in his wheelhouse. If he is willing, he will be perfect."

# CHAPTER 16

## A BEAUTIFUL GARDEN BEGINS TO GROW

It is two years later.

The intra-planetary dialog initiative has mushroomed to become magnificent. Thousands from one planet are sharing information with those of like interests on the other planet. The Aura governing board communicates regularly with the Idel senators. Mechanics are talking with mechanics, scientists with scientists, lawyers with lawyers and laborers with laborers. Credit belonged to Trussx for Idel's citizens' participation, and to Colonel Wise for Aura's. The Colonel had used his mentoring organization which had ties extending to every nook of Aura to draw people into the program. Trussx had enlisted each Senator who, in turn, worked through their political contacts to shape a robust operation on Idel. Full-time directors were needed for each planet, and we recruited two brainy and sociable professionals to manage and grow operations.

Growing out of these connections is a particularly noteworthy development. Dr. Auglas of Idel University is a most distinguished scientist and a proponent of green energy. An optimistic but practical problem solver, he had exceeded everyone else in experimenting and then publishing his scientific advances. Yet it went nowhere until Trussx learned of it.

She appointed me to oversee a project headed by Dr. Auglas, the cost of it coming from one of her budgets. Dr. Auglas was heading pools of top scientists from both planets to find a way to water and plant 300,000 square miles of pebbles and rocks on Idel. It was a large area and it had been an Idel vision for years to reclaim the land and try to make it become productive.

The area is far from human population. Its air is a thin, hot stationary blanket. The mission was to start plant life leading to humans living there.

Needed for growth is water which lies exceptionally deep under the surface. Also needed is energy to get the water to the surface. Once there, the water needed to be filtered and distributed widely.

Dr. Auglas believes there is water here if you go deep enough, and cited my experience with the bubbling spring, a story that has become well known on both planets. He and his colleagues have created powerful water sensor devices that can detect the location of water deep in the ground. Then hovering helicopters with the sharpest drill bits known to science and water-detection sensors at their tips grind down to find water. Pipe then is installed deep into the water operated by helicopters hovering above.

Using brawny mega batteries, water is initially pumped to tanks on tall stilts, positioned high above the ground. The energy of the mega batteries is renewed by the fall of captured water up in the tanks on stilts down water into reservoirs on the ground. Oxygenators that bring about quick and strong plant growth are added. From there, it is distributed either by pipes or by drones spreading the water where needed

The brilliant Dr. Auglas is an exceptionally quiet man who is so mild-mannered, you would never think he is a brilliant scientist who may have a lot to say.

Another shared project is one most everyone on both planets is anticipating: the shuttle between the two planets. It is a large 38-passenger spaceship with 25 suites and 18 lounge chairs. There is a large lounge with a chef offering food and drink. It will be operated by a commission equally representing both nations. Its cargo area is large enough to haul four large vehicles or one small aircraft. Flight time between the two planets is expected to be two days.

Trussx and Hotten were divorced 18 months ago. Trussx is more relaxed now and says she is learning how to have fun again. We meet every six weeks. When she is on Aura, she stays with me and keeps some of her clothes in my apartment. It just makes it easier. And I stay and keep some clothes at her place when I go to Idel.

Idel manufacturers requested a face-to-face conference with their fellow manufacturers on Aura to understand more about the value of clean energy. Trussx traveled with them for a week of green energy show-and-tell. There are more of these intra-planet learning and business development events.

In Aura restaurants, there can be found dishes made from popular Idel recipes, and vice versa. Both nations' travel industries have scoped each other's vacation spots.

Another year has passed. Idel is fast becoming greener as a nation. Every spaceship trip I take allows me to observe the clouds above Idel's industrial areas. Once black with smoke, they then turned grey, and now white. Aura experts have been helping with that. Further, many ways of Idel's production have been made more economical. Aura experts have been helping with that by talking regularly with their counterparts at Idel.

The cities are cleaner, the gardens brighter and the people laugh more.

Hotten has remarried. He and Trussx are friendly. She is happy for him.

The deluxe spaceship has been completed. It has taken six tests runs to double check all the systems. Planned is a longer test run for which both Trussx and I will be on board.

This deluxe shuttle is something for which Trussx has great pride. Under her leadership, the ship was conceived and became a reality.

It looks like a gargantuan glistening white whale tastefully trimmed in yellow when lying horizontally on the ground.

The day of the trip arrived. A crowd of several thousand had assembled to watch the takeoff. Along aboard were Dr. Auglas, Captain Cos, Colonel Wise, Major Hanshaw, Susan Darl, Professor Higrow and the members of the teams working on the Idel desert as well as the builders of the dazzling new spaceship.

We board, and are shown how to buckle ourselves into a special kind a seat that automatically moves into comfortable positions to account for both for the thrust and the vertical or horizontal levels of the craft.

# CHAPTER 17

## AND THERE WE WERE

Flight time between Planet Idel and Aura is two days, but today was our third day on board the spaceship. I find Major Hanshaw, who answers: "No. We are flying exactly as planned. To test the ship, we had to fly at various speeds and in different directions. There have been turns and speed differences you would not have noticed."

A physician on board examined me because I complained about shortness of breath. She said my body was likely reacting to the flight's duration and speed. It was a difficult trip for me; I was disoriented and felt out of sorts. What seemed like days later, I finally heard the announcement on board the spacecraft: "Please prepare for landing."

The spacecraft hovered, then landed. Tears welled in Trussx's eyes. She unbuckled from her seat, came over, and held onto me tightly. I could not speak. She stood up and she, Captain Cos, and Major Hanshaw came to help me stand. Every joint in my body seem to lose its purpose of connecting bones. With one on each side, the Captain and the Major held me steady as I tried to move one foot in front of the other. Trussx followed closely behind.

As I approached the doorway, I saw the ship had landed on a bright green lawn. As my eyes adjusted to the light, I saw trees and a flower garden. In the distance water was being pulled from the ground into tanks on those high towers.

The other passengers surround us as we stood, blinking. Colonel Wise addressed our group.

"Welcome to Planet Earth," he said. "This is a cooperative project between Idel and Aura to engineer the rebirth of Earth."

He gestured to the splendid green lawn. "This is the location where the Earth Apocalypse Museum will stand," he said. "It was the inspiration of Idel Senator Trussx. Construction is under her direction, and will tell the history of Earth and its Apocalypse.

"Trussx already has several artifacts in a metal box and believes the owner might be willing to loan it to the Museum. Its building, which is currently in design, is seen as the centerpiece attracting tourists from Aura and Idel. Financing is coming from the nations of both planets."

**I was in awe, as was everyone else.** People were communicating only by whispering. I reached down and touched the grass. Then pulled some and rubbed it on my face, then Trussx's. I turned to her and began crying like a baby.

Motorized carts appeared from a distance and space passengers began boarding.

I leaned into Trussx and began telling her how much I loved her. She responded with a kiss and we held each other tightly.

"Trussx, will you marry me?"

She choked out through tears: "Yes." We hugged tightly and kissed again.

I said "Let's build our home over there on that knoll. It will have big glass windows and we will be able to see for miles. It will be a summer home for you and me here on Earth."

We slipped over into the garden and I cut a yellow rose and gave it to her. We both had blazing smiles as we reentered the spaceship. Flowers now were everywhere. Champagne was being passed around. There was a four-layer cake topped with a United Nations flag and by now, everyone had crowded in the lounge. The laughter was happy and hearty.

"Where did all of this come from?" I asked.

No one answered. They all just looked at me and grinned then returned to the conversations they had been having. I heard someone standing behind ask softly: "Is it time to cut the cake?"

# CHAPTER 18

## AND THEN, THIS

I was up early the next day, elated with the thought of spending the rest of my life with Trussx and overjoyed by the renewal of Earth. Everyone else was sleeping but Dr. Auglas, who I found sitting alone in the lounge.

We greeted each other and I sat down. In hopes of having a morning discussion with a near stranger, across from him, I said, "I hear that a few people are planning to build permanent residences or summer homes on Earth."

"Yes," he said. "I heard that also."

"Would you be one of those?"

"Truthfully, no."

That surprised me. I could understand him simply saying "no" and leaving it there. He was the brilliant engineer who made the extraction of the water on both Earth and Idel possible. But when he said "truthfully," it turned from being courteous chit-chat to what may be something troublesome about settling on Earth. I wondered how I could learn more about what he knew without pressing him too hard.

"Your inventing the process of bringing water to the surface in Indel changed the planet as we know it," I said. "I understand much of it is due to your successful engineering innovation."

"I had the world's best team of engineers working alongside me," he said. "They deserve praise for their fine work."

"And you must be proud that you and your colleagues are duplicating your Idel initiative here."

His silence spoked volumes about something being very wrong,

Then he responded, "No, I am not."

I was speechless. Just gaped.

"I am confident the water sources for Idel will eventually produce enough water to support habitation of that planet's vast wasteland," he said. "I have no worries.

"I frankly am upset with the decision to reclaim Earth based solely upon the groundwater sizes of the three planets. They are all about the same. However, Earth no longer has melting snow, rainstorms

96

and the oceans that feed them since the apocalypse," he said. "I believe we would be lucky to get 40 years of water at most from the Earth's groundwater, which is its only source of water both now and in the foreseeable future."

Then he asked me, "Did it ever rain while you were in that canyon?"

I thought for a while and replied, "I do not believe so."

I sat numb. What he is saying was making sense. I asked, "Why doesn't anyone realize this?"

"I have been preaching it regularly at our staff meetings," he said. "This is a problem when you have too many – in this case, two planets – involved. I tried to tell this to many from both planets all the while being unsure who ultimately makes the decisions.

"Another problem: there was such a bright and powerful moonglow about this undertaking that no one wanted to believe the facts. People listened but it stopped there."

I asked, "What about that land currently being reclaimed, fertilized, water and seeded?"

"That is going to last no longer than the ground water lasts. Its worth is just a drop in the bucket, as the saying goes. It is difficult to realize that water makes up 71 percent of Aura and Idel, and about the same percentage of everything on Earth before the apocalypse. The vital importance of water is grossly underrated. And Earth doesn't have it."

I felt dazed as I thanked Dr. Auglas. Trussx was still sleeping. I awakened her with the news of what I had just learned. She hurriedly dressed and went to find Dr. Auglas. When she returned, her face was ashen.

I said, "We need to get the truth out immediately so that the public will hear it from us first. If they hear it elsewhere, they may question our candor. We need to convey what we know about Earth."

Trussx, tears silently running from her eyes, said what everyone already knew. "It was my idea to reclaim Earth. Both Idel and Aura spent billions on it."

She now was weeping. I put my arms around her and held her tightly. We sat down, alone. I gave her my handkerchief to dab at her tears.

Finally, she said, "As soon as we return to Idel, I will go to the government building and will hand to the clerk my letter officially resigning from the Senate, effective immediately."

"Trussx, are you certain you want to do that? You have been vitally important to both planets."

"It was the people who had trust in me," she said. "They were responsible for whatever was accomplished. Without them and without their trust, I have ... nothing," she said as she began trembling. "My new mission is to use whatever credibility I may have left to make everyone understand life will become increasingly tenuous on Earth and then ... impossible." She stopped, weeping convulsively, and finally pulled herself together and looked me in the eyes.

"Planet Earth will never be renewable, never fixable," she said.

# ABOUT THE AUTHOR

Dan Pinger has played many roles in his long and eventful life. He raises horses. He served in the U.S. Army. He was a notably indifferent law school student. As a newspaper reporter, he covered the wild and woolly days when the Mob ran Newport, Kentucky. He also spent some time in academia, working as an administrator at the University of Cincinnati. He founded the Dan Pinger Public Relations agency where he and the hundreds of "Pingerites" who worked with him offered communications counsel to clients across Cincinnati and the nation for more than 25 years. And of course, Dan is a father, a son, a husband, living through all the joy and heartbreak those roles bring.

Now in his late 80s, Dan has turned his creative energy to writing. He published his first book of poetry, *Love, Laughter, Life and the Hereafter*, in 2016 and his second book, *The Ripley Ridge Storyteller*, in 2017. His third compilation of poems, *The Ripley Ridge Raconteur*, was completed in 2018. He wrote *A Reporter's Memoir: When the Mob Ruled Newport* in 2019. *Black Smoke and Blind Men* is his first foray into fiction.

Made in the USA
Lexington, KY
29 October 2019